MEG MOG and OG

for Zac

MEG MOG and OG

by Helen Nicoll
and Jan Pieńkowski

PUFFIN BOOKS

Meg was making
bubble and squeak

Mog and Owl
were having a bat hunt

SPLAT

A bat
fell in
the pot

Meg
Mog
and Owl fell through
the
floor

Meg put the cauldron on the fire

There were drawings on the wall

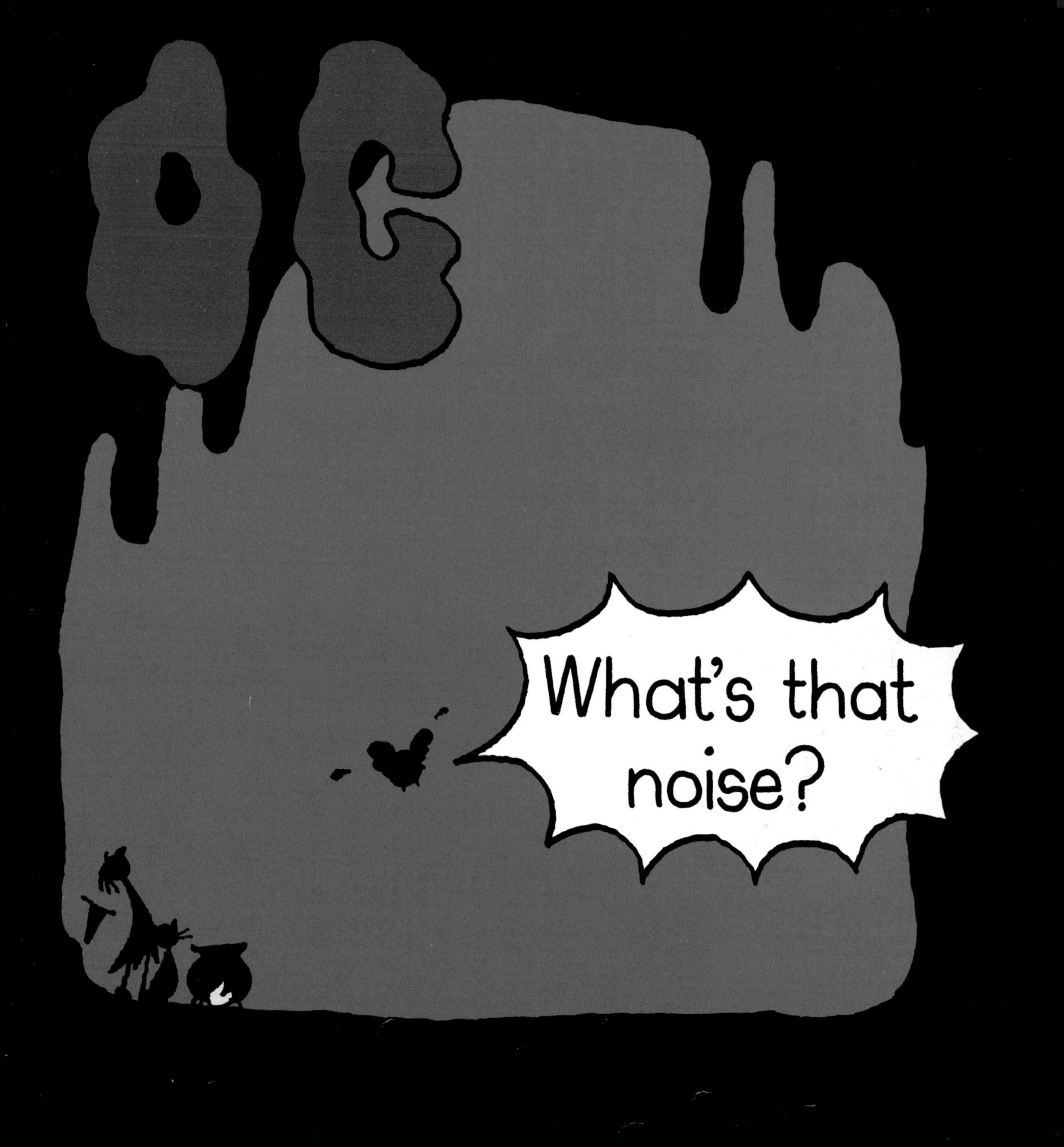
What's that noise?

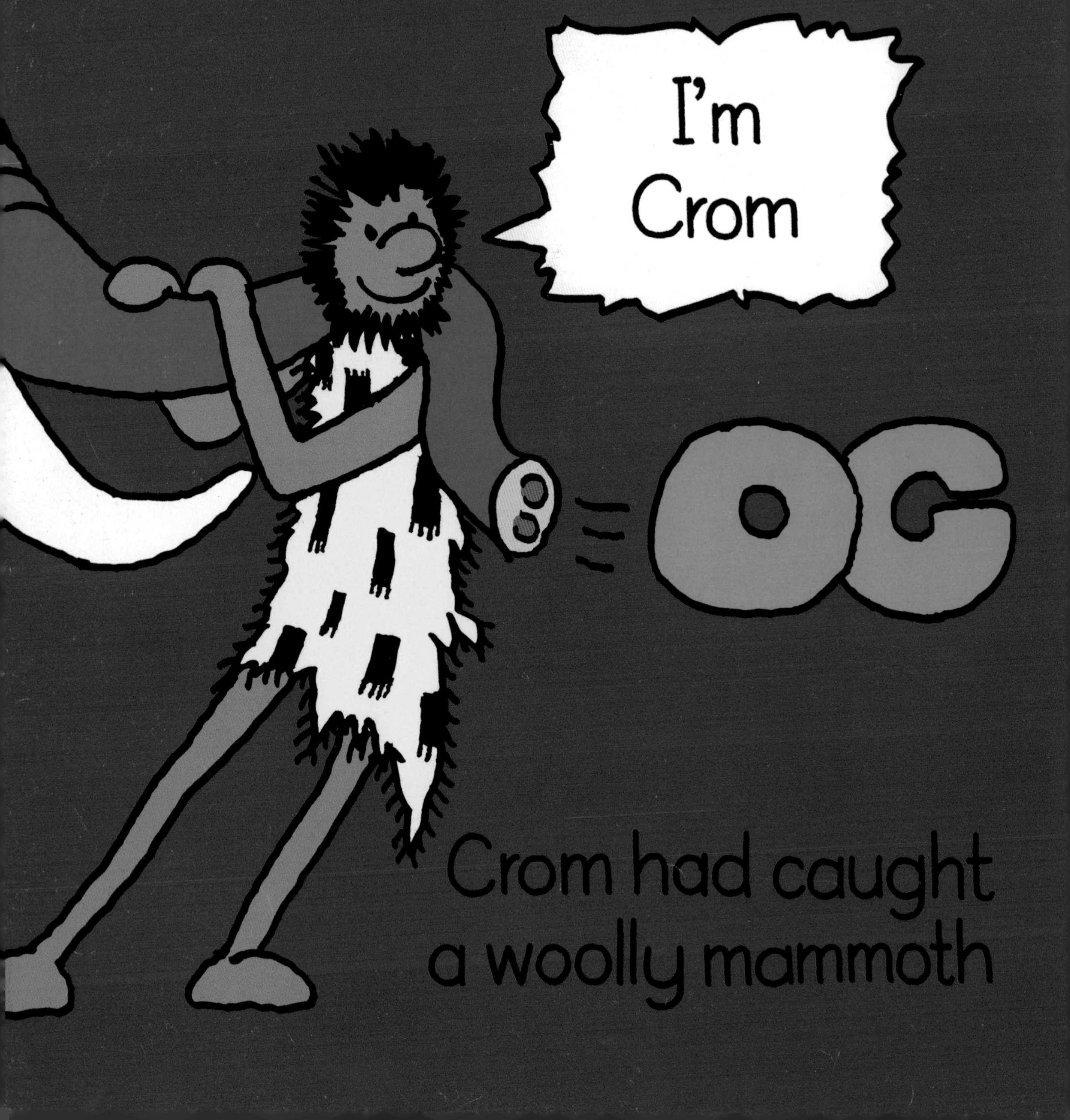

Crom had caught
a woolly mammoth

Crom liked
bubble and squeak

Every night
they slept on
the floor

It was very cold

Goodbye!